The OCEAN VOYAGES
of TRIM and
Captain FLINDERS
1799 ~ 1803

ASIA

PACIFIC OCEAN

INDIAN OCEAN

Kupang

In HMS Cumberland
1803

Isle de France

In HMS Reliance
1799

AUSTRALIA

Wreck Reef

TRIM the Cat
born in HMS Reliance

Port Jackson

In HMS Investigator 1801

In HMS Reliance
1800

INDIAN OCEAN

For KT ~ CF
For Steve Winn ~ CS

First published by Allen & Unwin in 2019

Allen & Unwin
83 Alexander Street
Crows Nest NSW 2065
Australia
Phone: (61 2) 8425 0100
Email: info@allenandunwin.com
Web: www.allenandunwin.com

A catalogue record for this
book is available from the
National Library of Australia

ISBN 978 1 76063 184 0

For teaching resources, explore
www.allenandunwin.com/resources/for-teachers

Cover and text design by Sandra Nobes
Set in 18 pt Old Claude by Sandra Nobes
This book was printed in November 2018 by C&C Offset Printing Co. Ltd, China.

1 3 5 7 9 10 8 6 4 2

*Historical records will always differ.
Every effort has been made to accurately tell this story.*

A Cat Called Trim

CORINNE FENTON

ILLUSTRATED BY CRAIG SMITH

ALLEN&UNWIN
SYDNEY · MELBOURNE · AUCKLAND · LONDON

Trim was a cat born for adventure. His life began on the sailing ship *Reliance*, somewhere in the southern Indian Ocean, bound for Botany Bay. Even as a tiny kitten Trim was more courageous, mischievous and fearless than his brothers and sisters.

HMS *Reliance*
1799

One night, Trim was tumbling and twirling about so vigorously
that *whoosh!*...off he went, slip-sliding over the side of the
ship and down, down, into the deep, dark water. Trim was
a tiny dot in a huge inky whirlpool. Every so often his head
popped to the surface, only to disappear again into the murky
depths. But someone was watching.

Matthew Flinders tossed in a rope and as fast as a musket ball
Trim shimmied up into his arms, his little heart pounding.
While Trim loved everyone on board,
it was Flinders he loved best of all.
Some animals choose their masters.
Trim chose Matthew Flinders.

Norfolk
1799

Sailing on the *Norfolk*, Trim met Bongaree,
who took special care of him. Animals
trust those who show kindness.

HMS *Reliance*
1800

On the high seas, danger was always close. Many ships were lost but, like his master, Trim loved sailing into unknown tomorrows, the wind in his hair. When 'Away up aloft' was called, he streaked up the rigging, reaching the top before any sailor.

Trim was always first at the officers' dinner table, nose twitching, waiting to be offered a tasty morsel. Then he would skulk away to the crew's quarters for second helpings. By the time the *Reliance* had returned to England, Trim had travelled the globe.

While Flinders attended to business, Trim was cared for by a kind lady. Life in a house was much the same as shipboard-life.

There were mice to catch, adventures
to be had, and the promise of affection at the
end of the day – even when he was naughty.

Trim packed his manners when he travelled by stagecoach to London with his master and when he greeted strangers along city streets. Trim believed all humans were his friends.

With orders to explore and chart the unknown southern coast of Australia, Flinders and Trim set off on the sloop *Investigator*. On the journey back to Port Jackson, Trim resumed his regular mousing duties, but also became the boss of several dogs. He chased them out of forbidden places, giving them a swipe on the nose when they disobeyed him.

HMS *Investigator*
1801

Only once was Trim a thief.
Scrumptious smells wafted
past his nose and about his
whiskers. He enlisted the
help of Van, a Dutch cat,
but the steward spotted them.
Although Van scampered away,
Trim stood tall to receive his punishment.

Later, with golden
eyes flashing, Trim
settled the debt.

HMS *Investigator*
1802

Sailing up the east coast of Australia and into the Gulf of Carpentaria, food was scarce and, like his master, Trim became thin and grey. With billowing sails, through storms and fierce winds, the ship swept down the west coast of Australia and across the Great Australian Bight.

HMS *Porpoise*
1803

On a dark, treacherous night in the Coral Sea, the sails of the *Porpoise* shook violently in ferocious winds and high breakers beat down upon her. She struck a coral reef. The *Porpoise* was shipwrecked.

Once again, like long ago, Trim was a tiny dot in a huge inky whirlpool. This time, Trim saved himself by scrambling out of the water and onto the reef.

The officers, crew and passengers recovered what
supplies they could and set up camp on the reef bank.
Flinders prepared to return to Port Jackson to organise
a rescue ship.

'But, you must stay here, old friend,' Flinders
whispered to Trim.

Time dragged, and Trim, steadfast, watched and waited.
Then one morning, there appeared a sail
on the far-away horizon.

With a chosen few, they headed
northward for England aboard the creaky,
leaky *Cumberland* – a small ship
for a huge journey.

HMS *Cumberland*
1803

The *Cumberland* was crawling with fleas, cockroaches and mice.
'Get to work on the mice, will you, Trim,' Flinders said.

In the Indian Ocean, not far from Trim's birthplace, the
Cumberland sailed into the unknown. Ahead could be
monsoons, hurricanes or even pirates – but they had
to take a chance.

With a leaking ship and only one struggling pump, Flinders made the fateful decision to call at the Isle de France for urgent supplies and repairs. Even though there was no choice, it was a decision he would always regret.

Upon arrival, Flinders was accused of spying.
His precious charts, books and journals were confiscated.
Flinders, along with Trim and another officer, were taken
prisoner and locked in a dingy room brimming with bed bugs
and buzzing mosquitoes.

While Flinders could not leave the stifling prison room, Trim escaped for regular night-time prowls into the town of Port Louis, stealing his way along its winding laneways. Trim was always watchful, ears pricked up, nose twitching, hugging the shadows as he crept.

Flinders worried about Trim. Where did his cat go
and who did he meet, when he vanished into the night?

Weeks then months of imprisonment dragged by,
and in the slow dawn light of one empty morning,
Trim did not return.

Flinders never saw Trim again, but he understood.
Some animals choose their masters, and some choose when
it's time to move on. Trim was a cat born for adventure,
and his next adventure had just begun.

Postscript

Trim stood with Flinders as they sailed the seaways of the world. Trim's loss made Flinders' darkest days darker.

Matthew Flinders remained a prisoner on Isle de France for many years. He died in London in 1814, the day after his life's work, *A Voyage to Terra Australis*, was published, and without realising his promise to build a statue in Trim's memory.

Today, several statues of Matthew Flinders with his loyal friend, Trim, stand around the world.

HMS *Reliance*   *Norfolk*   HMS *Investigator*   HMS *Porpoise*   HMS *Cumberland*

In HMS Cumberland 1803
to Isle de France

In HMS Investigator 1803

Kupang

TIMOR

NEW HOLLAND

Terra

In HMS Investigator 1801-02
from England

In HMS Reliance 1799
from Cape of Good Hope